Arriba

Arriba

Joe Cepeda

¡Me gusta leer!™

HOLIDAY HOUSE • NEW YORK

Para los Licano

¡Me gusta leer! is a trademark of Holiday House Publishing, Inc.

Copyright © 2016 by Joe Cepeda
Spanish translation © 2021 by Holiday House Publishing, Inc.
Spanish translation by Eida del Risco
All Rights Reserved
HOLIDAY HOUSE is registered in the U.S. Patent and Trademark Office.
Printed and bound in April 2021 at C&C Offset, Shenzhen, China.
The artwork was created with digital tools.
www.holidayhouse.com
First Spanish Language Edition
Originally published in English as *Up*, part of the I Like to Read® series.
I Like to Read® is a registered trademark of Holiday House Publishing, Inc.
1 3 5 7 9 10 8 6 4 2

Library of Congress Cataloging-in-Publication Data

Names: Cepeda, Joe, author, illustrator. | Del Risco, Eida, translator.
Title: Arriba / Joe Cepeda ; Spanish translation by Eida del Risco.
Other titles: Up. Spanish
Description: First Spanish language edition. | New York : Holiday House, [2021]
Series: ¡Me gusta leer! | Originally published in English in
2016 under title: Up. | Audience: Ages 4-8. | Audience: Grades K-1.
Summary: "On a very windy day, a boy stands by a window with his
pinwheel and is suddenly whisked into the sky where he can see a pig, a
hen, a cow, and a sheep"—Provided by publisher.
Identifiers: LCCN 2020030734 | ISBN 9780823449576 (trade paperback)
Subjects: CYAC: Winds—Fiction. | Domestic animals—Fiction. | Spanish language materials.
Classification: LCC PZ73 .C383 2021 | DDC [E]—dc23

ISBN: 978-0-8234-4957-6 (paperback)

Mira.

Mira.

Subo.

Veo una gallina.

Veo una oveja.

Veo una vaca.

Veo un cerdo.

Ellos van a casa.

Yo voy a casa.

¡Me gusta leer!

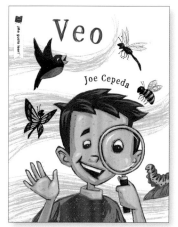

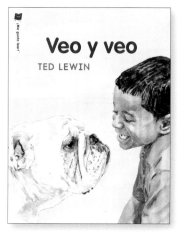

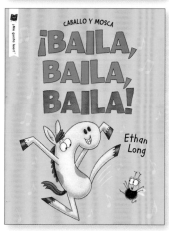

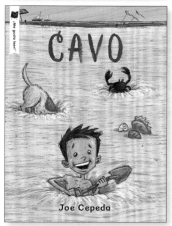

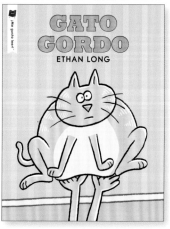